Shazira Shazam and the Devil

by
Erica and Guy
Ducornet

Prentice-Hall, Inc.
ENGLEWOOD CLIFFS, N.J.

to Jean-Yves

and to Kevin Page

Shazira Shazam and the Devil by Erica and Guy Ducornet © 1970 by Erica and
Guy Ducornet
Copyright under International and Pan American Copyright Conventions
All rights reserved. No part of this book may be reproduced in any form or by any
means, except for the inclusion of brief quotations in a review, without permission
in writing from the publisher.
ISBN: 0-13-807875-0
Library of Congress Catalog Card Number: 76-117552
Printed in the United States of America   J
Prentice-Hall International, Inc., London; Prentice-Hall of Australia, Pty. Ltd.,
Sydney; Prentice-Hall of Canada, Ltd., Toronto; Prentice-Hall of India Private
Ltd., New Delhi; Prentice-Hall of Japan, Inc., Tokyo

Once upon a time there lived an old man named Shazira Shazam who had never seen the world.

Sometimes he thought the world was round and sometimes he was certain that it was not—but it didn't really matter much. Simply, he was tired of home and longed for new places.

Every morning when he woke up he lay still in his bed and thought, "Today Shazira Shazam will go out and see the world!" But when he got up from his bed, his bones ached and his knees shook with age and he said, "Pooh! It's too late. You're an old man, Shazira Shazam!"

And so he sat sadly on his door-step watching the passersby, complaining to himself and cursing the sun and the good winds.

One day as he was sitting on his step, he saw a very old and dusty camel limping down the street. And he thought to himself, "That camel is surely as old as I, and yet see how he manages to get about. The devil take me! I bet that dusty hump has seen more of the world than I!"

That night, Shazira Shazam had a very strange dream. He dreamed that the devil himself stood before him, and that he had a great hump on his back. "Why, he's just like a camel!" Shazira said to himself, and he began to laugh.

"Hee hee hee!" cried Shazira.

"Hee hoo hee!"

The devil laughed too, making Shazira laugh harder— so hard that the tears streamed down his face and the very walls of the room shook.

"Hee hee hee!" sobbed Shazira.

"Hee hee haw!" screamed the devil.

But then all at once the devil stopped laughing and with one quick, nimble bound, sat hunched by Shazira's ear.

"Hey there, Shazira Shazam," he whispered hotly between chuckles into Shazira's ringing ear. "So—you'd like to see the world—become a traveling man, eh?"

"*O yes!*" breathed Shazira, his eyes as bright as two gold coins.

"Well then," cried the devil. "Hop on. Hop on my hump and I'll show you around. Hurry, Shazira. There isn't much time!"

Shazira was just about to leap up on the devil's hump when the morning sun broke, and he found himself alone and wide awake.

"O Pooh," he cried. "Zarn and tarnish! I've missed the ride! Now I'll never see the world."

So, Shazira had some mint tea and then went out to sit on his front step as was his habit. He hadn't been sitting for long when he saw the same old camel limping down the street. Shazira scratched his head and thought a bit and said, "Well, maybe it's temptation, and then again, maybe it isn't. But I think that camel is meant for me, and I'm going to take a ride."

The camel must have been a mind-reader because he crossed right over and stood before Shazira, rolling his eyes and sticking out his tongue. "Hop on," he said.

"Well, thanks," said Shazira, "don't mind if I do!" and *hop,* there he was sitting on the camel's back as if it were the most natural thing in the world.

And then Shazira began to laugh. "Hee hee hee! Hee hee ho!" And the more he laughed, the faster the camel ran. *"Hee hee hee!"* Shazira couldn't stop, and trees and houses and dogs and people and cows and barns and rivers whirred past so quickly that he couldn't make out any of it.

"Heeee hee heeee," cried Shazira as the sun spilled past and the moon went soaring. He laughed as the stars whistled above his head, schools of birds tangled in his beard, his nose blew like an engine, and as the clouds whipped into cream.

Night and day and day and night shot past like the blinking of an eye, and the camel kicked up a path of dust as high as the sky.

They flew like the wind and Shazira wondered if a thousand days were passing or one minute—whether the world was round or not—and if he were a man or a devil.

"Devil!" he cried. "Devil!" and at once the camel stopped short and sent Shazira spinning to the ground. The old camel had a mean glint in his eye. Shazira looked into the camel's eyes hard and long. "Yep," he sputtered. "Devil. Not a true camel at all. Well! I know your game." But he wasn't sure that he did. He sat down, not very surprised that he sat on his very own front step, and scratched his head.

"Well," he said at last. "I suppose that you expect something in return for the ride."

"The usual price," the camel drooled, "is a soul."

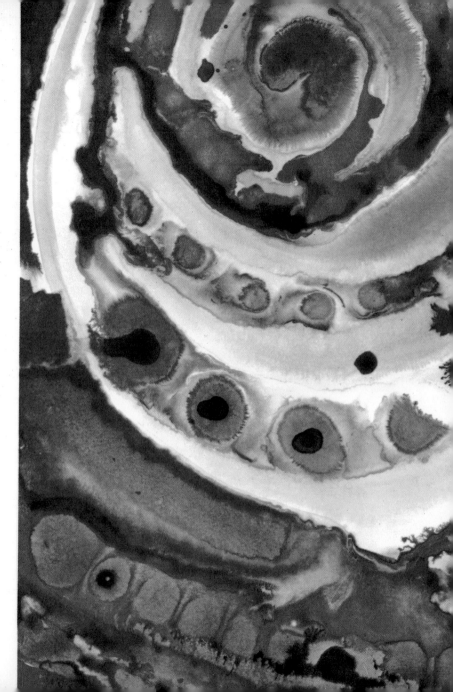

Shazira trembled from head to foot, scratched his head and thought as fast as his old brains would allow. Then he said, "Tell me this, your honor," (the camel snickered) "a devil's hump is a pretty permanent thing, is it not?"

"Weeelll yeeess," the devil replied, a bit peeved in the face.

"I could rid you of it," said Shazira, "for a price."

"Hah," said the devil. "Hah!"

"It's true," said Shazira. "This may surprise you, I know, but I've erased many a hump in the past and I don't see why yours should be different." "You'd make quite a hit with the ladies without it," he added hopefully.

Clearly this last remark touched the devil's heart. He began to "Hmmmmm" and "Hmmmmm" in a most promising manner. And he "hmmmmmed" some more. "Well, it's a deal," he said at last.

"Good!" said Shazira, his heart pounding. "Good! Come tomorrow morning. I need some time to get things ready."

So the devil went tottering down the street and Shazira ran to the money box hidden under his bed. Inside glowed ten pieces of gold—the pleasure of his old age.

He put the gold into his pocket
and went to speak with his
neighbors: Cramcrust the butcher,
Zacheal the baker, Ripzatch the
tailor, Stagnet the juggler, Favida
the cook, Bravda the beauty and
Pooltub the philosopher.

To each he said, "Will you do me a small favor?" as the gold glistened in his hand. And when they saw the gold, their eyes shone and their palms itched.

"Dear friend and beloved neighbor," they cried. "Just speak. We will gladly do what you wish!"

"All that I ask," said Shazira, "is that you agree with whatever I say tomorrow, no matter how foolish it may be." And they agreed.

Well, the next morning at the rooster's cry, the devil came limping down the street until he stood before Shazira's door.

"Come in!" cried Shazira. "Sit down before the fire, dear."

"Gladly," said the devil, touched by the affectionate greeting. "Fire is what I like best."

Then Shazira took a great pot from the fire, steaming with milk and rice, and poured it over the devil's hump.

"*Ooooohhh!*" breathed the devil. "How *good* it feels!" And he sighed.

Then Shazira danced around
the room and chanted,
"Saloma
SALoma
Bazoma

DRABOMA
Dromdoma
Dromdoma

ZWACK!
ZWACK!
ZWACK!

Well . . . there you are!"

"There I'm *where*?" asked the camel.

"Well it's gone," said Shazira. "The hump is gone. It's an old remedy passed on by my grandmother, and it's worked as it always does."

"Pooh," said the devil. "I can still feel it."

"Only your imagination," said Shazira. "It will take awhile for you to get used to being without it. But I assure you—it's gone—quite gone."

The devil craned his neck and tried to see and thought he saw the hump and said so.

"Nonsense," cried Shazira. "You simply see your back. Come, to prove it to you, we will go out into the street and ask my neighbors."

Shazira and the camel stepped outside. At that moment, Bravda was passing and Shazira called, "Bravda, come and see this handsome horse!"

"Indeed!" cried Bravda. "It looks more like a camel."

"Hah," said the devil. "Just as I thought."

"But silly Bravda," Shazira insisted. "Camels have *humps*! This creature has none." Bravda, who could have kicked herself, remembered the gold and answered, "But of course, Shazira. You're so right—it *is* a horse, not a camel at all! Who's ever seen a camel without a hump?"

By this time, the others had gathered around Shazira and the devil and were earnestly agreeing. "Yes . . . indeed . . . a horse . . . a *handsome* horse . . . such a fine strong back it has . . . a magnificent beast . . ." and so on.

The devil was not accustomed to such fuss and admiration, and he was feeling good and even grateful to Shazira. So when at last the neighbors had departed, he turned to Shazira and said, "Well, then, you've been true to your word, Shazira Shazam, and I will be true to mine. Your soul is yours—until the next time."

"Honorable and pleasant devil!" cried Shazira. "I do believe your word. But—forgive me—I am but a humble man and would, ah, appreciate some token, some proof that my soul is mine to keep."

"Quite right," said the devil. "Pluck a hair from my hump—that will be proof of our agreement."

Shazira stretched to pull the hair from the camel's hump. But as soon as his fingers touched it they stuck like glue.

Once again the devil took Shazira Shazam for a ride . . .

. . . and as the wind whistled past
and the dust flew fast and thick and
the sun glowed hot and red, Shazira
could hear the devil's laughter.